Pressure Drop

With love,
Amanda
S x

Amanda Saint

Contents

Peeling Away All The New Layers

Compelled to leave as soon as she'd put the phone down, Stephanie had driven through the night. Leaving Ryan sleeping. He'd be angry when he woke but she couldn't worry about him now anyway. For once, he'd have to deal with her putting herself first. If coming back here could be called that.

Walking up the hill to the tiny chapel, the sun peeping over the hills behind her, her breath billowed, enshrouding her in a frosty mist. If only Diane had died in the summer. If Stephanie had to be back here after all this time, she'd rather it had been in the warm weather. But Diane never did like to make things nice for anyone.

'Don't call her that,' Stacey said last night when she'd called.

'It's her name.'

'She's our mum … was our mum.'

Freezing it might be, but at least it would be quiet. No tourists at this time of year. Or maybe that was all different now that Verity lived here. Stephanie glanced back at her, towering over the harbour entrance with her bronze sword held high. She looked normal from this side; it was her other side that caused so much controversy, the one facing out to sea. As if she could only reveal her true nature to the elements. Although why everyone, mainly men, were so upset by her insides, and the baby she carried, being on show, Stephanie just couldn't fathom. Maybe because it's the English way to keep everything at a surface level. Or maybe because it shows that women are the true creators, that without them there'd be nothing.

Stephanie paused at the chapel door. They'd spent so much time in here as kids, sheltering from the wind and rain when they didn't want to go home. Or couldn't. This was the first place where Stephanie had taken proper photos, the ones that made her believe she could make a career with her camera. Sunbeams slicing through the windows illuminating the altar, dust in the air. Everything else shrouded in shadow. She'd been so excited when she'd had the film developed and seen what she'd captured. Not that it had led anywhere in the end.

The door creaked as she pushed it open, and the familiar smell of wood and old paper surrounded her. Would the carving of her and Stacey's initials still be here? The two letters entwined. Like they'd thought they too always would be. Through the gloom, the shape of a man appeared as he sat up on one of the pews near the

front, rubbing sleep from his eyes. A dog growled next to him. Stephanie backed out, letting the door swing shut behind her.

Pink clouds scudded across the sky and the wind blew her hair across her face as she looked down at the waves crashing on the rocks below. Hopefully the man and his dog would leave now she'd woken them up. She could have the quiet time she needed to dig deep inside herself and find the courage to go back to that house. To see Stacey for the first time since she'd left. Sixteen years ago. How had all that time passed?

The chapel door creaked then she felt something touching her legs. A scruffy little brown and white dog was sniffing at her jeans. It looked up at her, then sat on her foot. She smiled, crouched, and held her hand for it to sniff. The dog gave it a quick lick.

'Sorry. He's just very friendly,' a gruff voice said.

Stephanie stood and turned. The man, in crumpled army fatigues, gave a wary smile. A real soldier or pretend? His hair and beard were scruffy too, and brown and white just like his dog.

'Well, I'm not.' She'd meant it to sound jokey but could hear the harshness as soon as the words were formed.

'We'll leave you be then. Jerry.' He patted his leg and the dog trotted straight to him. They disappeared around the first bend of the steep winding path back down to the harbour. Seconds after they did, she heard the patter of paws and expected Jerry to reappear. Instead, a whole posse of dogs did, followed by two women, a

man and four kids. What was everyone doing up here so early? Nobody ever used to come here.

The kids ran straight into the chapel while the adults came and stood alongside her, clutching coffee shop cups and chattering loudly to each other as if she wasn't even there. Stephanie headed down the path. Clearly she wasn't going to get any time alone. But she couldn't go back to the house yet. She wasn't ready. Wasn't sure she could go at all despite the midnight dash to get here.

The man who'd been in the chapel had stopped just ahead of her at the bottom of the hill. The dog was sniffing the weeds growing round the bottom of the sea wall but ran over when he spotted her, jumping up and putting both paws on her shins. She ruffled his head.

'Jerry. Down.'

'It's alright. Sorry about what I said. I am friendly really.' She didn't know why, but she really needed him to know that she wasn't that snappy, standoffish person. She just wasn't feeling quite herself at the moment. Being back here was peeling away all the new layers she'd swaddled herself in since leaving.

The man nodded but didn't really look at her. He patted his leg again and then he and Jerry marched off in the direction of town. She couldn't blame him for not wanting to talk to her.

Stephanie wandered on to the pier overlooking the harbour. The tide was creeping in. She watched it slowly lift the stranded boats until they were bobbing gently in

the shallow water. Waiting until it was deep enough so they could depart again.

A fisherman climbing onto his boat waved at her. In greeting or farewell, she couldn't tell.

Same, Same But Different

A shiny veneer had been painted over the town. One made of galleries and cafes starring artful driftwood. Bistros with Michelin stars and food that the locals definitely couldn't afford. Well not when she'd lived here anyway. Who knows nowadays? But some of the old places were still clinging on, behind grimy window displays where balls of wool were bundled in bins and second-hand chairs looked on the verge of collapse. These shops showed that underneath the gloss, the town was still the same.

Stephanie walked slowly, wending her way back to the house the long way round. Postponing this final step of her return for as long as she could. On the High Street faded memories rose and bubbled through her mind, before popping into technicolour high-definition replays.

The butcher's shop where she'd go with Stacey once a month clutching the note scrawled in Diane's messy hand. Without enough money to buy all the things on the list. Big Jim the owner, with his smiling blue eyes and crinkly face making his bloody apron a bit less scary, who'd always let them have it all anyway.

The old cinema where her and Emma would go as often as they could. Emma's mum paying for the both of them most times. Stumbling down the steps swooning with teenage lust after the first time seeing *Dirty Dancing*. Going to see it again and again and again. Practicing the moves in Emma's bedroom, wanting all the boys to want them that much, to sweep them out of this remote corner of Devon.

The rough old pub where her and Stacey would have to go and find Diane in the school holidays when there'd been no food in the house for days and days. And their dizzy brains and concave bellies just couldn't take it anymore.

The corner shop where the old woman who always wore bright red lipstick that bled into the wrinkles around her mouth, would let her and Emma buy bottles of cider when they were only fifteen.

The bench in the churchyard gardens where they'd sit and drink them, dreaming and planning how they could escape. Before spinning around and around and around, arms in the air, until they'd get so dizzy they'd collapse in a laughing heap on the grass.

The road where she'd lived.

No putting it off any longer.

The terraced house she grew up in.

Paint peeling on the window frames. The window in the front door with the same crack in it. Weeds poking up out of the path and the cracked concrete in the front yard. The scruffiest house in the street by far.

Nothing has changed.

The place where she grew her dreams and had them smashed. Where she loved and laughed, fought and flailed. Screamed and shouted. Hid and hugged.

The place she tried so hard to forget.

She swallowed, squeezed her eyes shut and gripped the gate.

She'd thought she was different, that the years away had changed her. But now she knows that, inside, she's still the same.

Reunion

Stephanie looked out through the kitchen window, unnoticed by Stacey who was sitting in a filthy orange deckchair, barefoot, wearing just a dressing gown, surrounded by empty bottles of gin and cans of cider. And was that a bong? Stacey was smoking a cigarette ferociously, muttering and sniggering, gesturing towards the empty deckchair next to her. Just as if Diane was still alive, sitting next to her and joining in the conversation. Is this how they had been spending their time before Diane died? Sitting around getting pissed and stoned.

Pushing the back door open, Stephanie huddled her face deeper into her scarf, her heart pulsing in her throat. Maybe it wasn't too late to run away again.

Stacey looked up. 'It's your fault,' she said. Her eyes skidded across Stephanie's without really meeting them.

Maybe Stacey was right. Maybe everything was Stephanie's fault for leaving them her and Diane behind. For wanting to in the first place.

She shuddered.

Stepped backward.

The Faultline Between Future and Past

Stephanie loitered on the landing, unable to venture inside the bedroom she'd slept in from birth until she was twenty-four. Taking a deep breath, she pushed the door open. The winter sunshine failed to brighten up how dismal it was. The room had been underexposed to light for far too long. The flimsy duvet, which never kept her warm, barely covered the sagging mattress. The echoes of Diane's shouts and Stephanie's screams still reverberated in the holes in the walls. Abandoned photography books on the bedside table covered in cobwebs and dust. Eyes watering at the smell, she covered her face with her arm and breathed through her sleeve. It's as if nobody ever went in the room again after she'd left.

Downstairs, the front door slammed.

Her chance to escape. She ran down the stairs, pulling her phone from her pocket. The front door key came with it and clanked onto the hallway floor. She left it there. Why had she kept it all these years anyway?

In the car she scrolled through lists of B&Bs. Maybe somewhere up the coast a bit, out of town, would be better. Ilfracombe was too full of the past.

A sharp rap on the window made her yelp and drop the phone in her lap. Stacey peered in gesturing for her to wind the window down. Stephanie pressed the button. If only she'd driven off before looking for a room.

'Where are you going?' Stacey's breath was rancid as she leaned in.

'I thought it would be better if I got a hotel. I can't sleep in my old room.'

Stacey snorted. 'Not up to your standards anymore, Miss Fancy Pants?' Bottles clinked together as the bag Stacey carried banged against the car door.

Stephanie shook her head. She didn't want a row. Especially in the street. That was always Diane's way. 'It's just for the best. I'll ring in the morning. Come round then and we can talk.' She pressed the button and the window closed.

Stephanie could feel Stacey's eyes upon her all the way to the end of the road. As she turned the corner, the aperture closed. The street where she grew up vanished, along with her sister.

Freedom Is A Cider-Fuelled Fantasy

On the news they've been banging on about global warming being a bad thing but bring it on, Stephanie says. Hot and sunny is definitely a good thing. She only has to stay here for two more summers after this then, once her A-levels are done, she'll escape to Central St. Martin's and start her new life as a photographer. She'll make the most of living by the beach while she can.

She grabs Emma by the hand, swinging her up and round, kicking up sand. 'We're going to be free, free, free, you and me!'

Ever since they were five, they've always done everything together. London next.

She lets go of Emma and grabs the cider, swigs it straight from the bottle. They pass it back and forth, gulping it until it's gone then collapse onto the picnic blanket, giggling.

'Where the hell have you been?' The words blare right down the road at her as soon as Stephanie turns the corner, sobering her immediately. She hurries towards the house. Best to get Mum inside, whatever it is. But it's too late, she's hurtling towards Stephanie, her red face writhing with rage. What now?

She grips Stephanie's upper arm and squeezes hard. 'I know what you've been planning and there's no way. No way.'

Spittle sprays across Stephanie's cheek. She wrenches her arm away. 'What are you on about now?'

'Bumped into Mr Swanky Art Teacher, didn't I? Telling me all about how talented you are, how glad he is you'll be doing it at A-level and going on to university. No way.'

Bony fingers jab at Stephanie's shoulder. She flinches.

'School's finished. You're getting a job. I'm sick of having to pay for everything. If you think you're just going to swan around for years taking bloody pictures.' She's tripping over her own feet as she chases Stephanie up the road, screeching for all the neighbours to hear.

Stephanie runs in and up to her room. Slams the door, as if that would keep her Mum out. No chance. It flings open, the door handle knocking another chunk out the wall.

'Think you're so special don't you, missy. Better than me.'

'It's my life. I should be able to do what I like with it.' Stephanie's voice cracks. Why does she always cry? She swallows the lump burning in her throat.

'I'm your mum. You do what I say. Always.'

'Well, you should have acted like a mum, Diane. Looked after me properly. Then maybe I'd want to tell you things, stick around.'

Diane shoves Stephanie in the chest. She falls backwards onto the bed. Watches Diane slam out of the room. The door opens again seconds later and Stacey slinks in. Lies down next to Stephanie on the bed and cuddles up to her as if they're little kids again. 'You wouldn't really go away and leave me here on my own, would you?' she whispers into Stephanie's ear.

Dread settles like lead in Stephanie's stomach.

Truly Deathly

Stephanie had forgotten how truly deathly it was round here in the winter. No shops or cafés open in the parade facing the beach. The only place welcoming customers was the massive new Wetherspoons. She couldn't go in there. That would be even more depressing than being indoors with stay-at-home Stacey.

The tide was way out, the sea flat, dull, grey. One of those days when everything felt too still, too heavy, as if the cold and the clouds could press her right down into the ground. Even the neon lights from the amusement arcade seemed muted, as did the jingles and crashes from the machines inside.

She'd walk up the hill to the flagpole to get warm. She couldn't go back to the house again yet. It was as if the nicotine-stained walls were stealing her breath. The raggedy old furniture and peeling wallpaper dragging her back to the past.

The path snaked upwards alongside the beach and as she reached the first bend, the one where Diane had died falling from the railings, a woman appeared coming the other way. Her hood was up so Stephanie couldn't see her face but, somehow, she knew who it was.

When they drew level, the woman spoke. 'Steph. I thought it was you. My God. It's been so long.' She stepped forward and pulled Stephanie into a hug. 'How are you?'

'Emma! How lovely. I'm good, how about you?' She pulled back from the hug before Emma noticed her wince. The bruises on her arm, where Ryan had gripped her to try and stop her leaving, were tender still. He worried what coming back here would do to her. And she was starting to think that maybe he was right to be concerned. She was certainly feeling off kilter.

Emma reached out and grabbed her hand. 'Sorry about your mum. You're back for the funeral?'

Stephanie nodded. Had her memories of Emma conjured here? Longing and nostalgia swelled in her as she smiled into Emma's eyes. Why hadn't they spoken for years?

'I'm sorry we lost touch when I moved back home. Why did you stay away so long?' Emma asked. No judgement in her voice, just curiosity it seemed.

Stephanie bit her lip, turned to face out to sea. Why did she? She cleared her throat. Could she tell Emma? Even after all this time? Emma did know what Stephanie had run away from. Had helped her escape. Was the best friend she'd ever had, even if they hadn't spoken in recent times.

'I was scared.' A shiver ran through Stephanie. That was the first time she'd said it out loud. But now she realised – she'd been needing to say it for a long time.

'Scared of what?' Emma joined her at the sea wall, gazed down at the beach below, as if she knew Stephanie could only speak if she didn't look at her.

'That I'd break the spell. It seemed like magic that I'd got away. Like it could never happen twice. I did think about visiting. But something told me if I did, I'd be stuck here for good. Like Stacey.'

'Stacey made her own choices. She could have left too,' Emma said.

Stephanie shook her head violently, gripped the railing as if she would wrench it from the rocks and throw it out to sea. 'No. There was only ever going to be one of us that got away. And it was always going to be me.'

'How can you know that?'

Stephanie prised her fingers from the railings and stuffed her hands in her pockets, taken aback at the force of her reaction. 'Because I was the one who always said no and Stacey always said, "*Yes, Mum. Of course, Mum*". No matter how crazy Diane's demands got, Stacey always did as she was told.'

Emma turned, patted Stephanie's arm. 'Well, it's all over now. Isn't it? Diane's gone. Come see me. We'll go for a drink. I'm living at my mum's, so you know where to find me.'

Stephanie smiled, 'I will. How is your mum?'

Emma shrugged. 'Good days and bad. But they said she'd be in a wheelchair by now and she's still walking around. With sticks mostly but still, walking is walking.'

'And how are you? Are you okay with being back here?'

'I wasn't for ages, but I am now. How could you not be okay with all this?' She waved her arm out to encompass the sea, the beach, the cliffs. 'Much nicer than the dirt and noise of London. See you soon, yeah.' She turned back to the path.

Stephanie watched her walk away until she vanished round the corner, then carried on walking up the hill. When she reached the flagpole, she climbed up on the rocks surrounding it, panting but no longer cold. She flung her arms above her head and waved them wildly in the wind that was picking up, as if they were sails and the breeze could carry her away. Would she want to be carried back to London and Ryan though? She wasn't sure. But there were other places she could go.

Down on the beach waves were slapping onto the shingle now, shifting it around, dragging some of it away and sending it elsewhere. But the big boulders stood resolute, unmoved by the winds and the water for centuries. Going nowhere.

No Going Back

Stephanie hugs her backpack to her as she sits on the hill looking back at the town and harbour — the only home she's ever known. Freezeframing it in her mind so she can look at it again when she needs to. Everything she wants to keep is in this bag. Everything she's been, or has wanted to be, is staying behind. Including her camera. Diane killed that dream stone dead. It's way too late to go to college now. That boat left eight years ago. Sailing for London without her on it. Leaving her here to pick up the pieces of all the dreams that Diane keeps smashing. Well, this time she really is done with it. The chapel's bells jangle into life – as if they're saying goodbye, good luck, God speed. Knowing the chapel won't need to give her a place to hide anymore.

It will probably take Diane days to realise she hasn't seen her, and Stacey will be so busy meeting her every demand she won't notice either. Well, they're welcome to each other. Stephanie blinks back the tears she's determined not to cry. Stacey will notice, of course she will. Is she doing the right thing leaving her behind? But she can't support Stacey too. She'll tell her sister to join her once she's settled and found a job. A place for both of them to live.

She inhales a waft of diesel from the fishing boats and the salty air infused with vinegar from the chip shops lining the harbour road. The smells of home. What will her new home smell like? She can't imagine anywhere that isn't here.

Hefting her backpack over her shoulders, Stephanie turns then follows the path further up the hill. It glows silver in the light of the rising moon, like a slug trail, showing her the way out instead of the way home. Emma's picking her up at the car park at the top. Giving her a place to stay in London for a while until she gets herself sorted out.

As she reaches the top of the path, a cloud covers the moon and the path she's just walked disappears into darkness.

Things To Sort For
The Funeral

Find cheapest option — of course Diane didn't have any savings to pay for her own funeral. Stacey said it's down to me seeing as I'm "*the one with the fancy London life and my own business*". As if running a little café would ever make me rich. Give me more than the bare minimum needed to scrape by in London. If the garden wasn't all concreted over, I'd be up for just digging a hole and dropping Diane in.

Flowers — done my research. Order bouquet of:

- Aconite – sign of danger and a need for caution.
- Striped carnations – very pretty but they mean rejection, refusal.
- Petunias – anger and resentment.

- Frog Orquid – disgust. At Diane. At Stacey for never standing up for herself. At all of us for the sorry, sordid story that is our family. Stacey will no doubt order Astilbes – dedication to a loved one. She was always the good daughter. The one who stuck around.

Tell Diane's friends — if she even has any, Stacey can do this. She's the one who has any clue what Diane's life has been for the past sixteen years.

Tell Ryan. Do I want him to come? Do I want him at all? Do I know anything anymore about how things will be from now on? I'll wait until the bruises have faded to decide.

Buy booze — lots of it. All the booze in all the shops. It's the only way I can get through this. Being here. Stacey's dead eyes following me everywhere. The sense that the past is reclaiming me. Burying the person I've become.

The Bad Daughter

The label seems to have been hers forever.

Being the bad daughter encompassed many wrong doings but her main transgressions were:

- *Always putting herself first.* Translation: trying to have a life of her own. Planning a future, having ambitions, wanting to see if a world existed beyond the Devon border. But being too scared to stand up to Diane until it was too late, and she'd lost her chance to do what she really wanted.
- *Never thinking about how her actions would affect Diane.* Translation: everything is always about Diane. Everything. Always. And if you did something to try and please her, based on what she'd wanted the day before, then that wouldn't be the right thing anymore. Whatever you did, it was always wrong.

- *Being a bad influence on her sister.* Translation: being the one who looked after her, fed her, got her to school, washed her clothes, held her when she cried at night about mummy not loving her. Feeling so terrible when she left her behind.
- *Not doing as she's told.* Translation: refusing to abide by Diane's ridiculous drunken demands. Of which there were many. Ever-changing. Often humiliating.
- *Dressing "like a tart".* Translation: wearing baggy black clothes to try and escape the leers and gropings dished out by Diane's ever-changing parade of boyfriends. Thinking that it was her job to make sure her outfits didn't provoke them. Not that what she wore made any difference at all.

Now that Diane is dead is she no longer the bad daughter? Is she even a daughter at all?

Home

The photo album's sticky pages had yellowed, bathing the images they held in a sickly glow. Stephanie wasn't sure why she'd brought the album with her to the pub today. Maybe because when Stacey had given it to her last night, she'd been so righteous, 'See she wasn't as bad as you think. She did love us.'

Beaming up from the page was a Polaroid of the three of them sitting on a green tartan blanket on the town beach, which Stephanie could see through the window now. Stephanie was about five, Stacey four, meaning Diane would have been that mythical age where real adulthood apparently begins. Twenty-one.

In the picture Diane was clinging to her little girls, laughing. Her hair blown in her eyes by the summer breeze. This would have been before their dad had left. He must have taken the photo. A badly composed, but beautifully candid shot that captured Diane completely unaware. She looked…young, happy, carefree. Her face wasn't yet ravaged by bitterness and vitriol. Her body not yet bloated with the booze and food she'd consume as if someone was going to take it away from her.

Stephanie had no doubt that Diane had loved her when she was this tiny little doll, completely dependent on her. Unquestioning, pliable, unable to get away.

The sound of the pub door opening made her look up. Instead of Emma, a soldier stood in the doorway. Behind him snowflakes swirled frantically in the wind. It took her a moment to realise it wasn't the army arriving to evacuate everyone ahead of the storm, The Beast from the East, as the media were hyping it up. It was the man she'd seen sleeping in the chapel on the morning she arrived. Where was his dog?

As if her question had summoned him, the dog appeared in the doorway. As did Emma who bent down and ruffled his head. 'Hello Jerry. Good boy.'

The soldier moved into the pub to allow Emma through the door and she patted him on the shoulder, 'Alright Adam? How you doing?'

He smiled and nodded, 'Not too bad. You know.'

Emma gave his shoulder a rub. 'Come round for a cuppa. Or for your tea. You know you can come whenever you like.' She walked over to Stephanie, reaching over for a hug before sitting down next to her.

'Who's that?' Stephanie said.

'Adam Chambers. You must remember him,' she winked.

Now Stephanie recalled a cocky, golden-haired boy surrounded by admirers, male and female. Her among them. She had to look again at this grizzled man with sad eyes standing waiting at the bar. Surely this was not the same person.

Emma leaned in, whispered, 'He was in Iraq and Afghanistan. Left the army and came back to look after his mum when she got sick. When she died the council took the flat back and he's been homeless ever since.'

Stephanie watched him as he took his pint to a small table by the fire, Jerry hot on his heels.

Homeless in his hometown.

Teenage Dreams

22nd May 1993

Dear Diary,

I am SO embarrassed. I can never go out, or to school, again. Me and Emma went to the disco in Hele Bay tonight. Our first time as we had to wait for Emma to turn 14, as everyone knows everyone around here and they're so square they wouldn't let her in even if it was just the day before her 14th birthday. So even though I've been able to go for five months, I waited for Emma. And we were so excited and it was so awful. I can never go back. Adam Chambers was there. ♥ ♥ ♥

And even though I've never told anyone apart from you and Emma that I like him, I went and told him. I could die. I was drunk. Also for the first time. I don't think I like it. I won't be doing that again.

Adam was with all his mates but the cider made me not care what they'd think and I went right over there and asked him to dance with me. A slow dance. What was I thinking? And it was to that really shit song by Phyllis Nelson that Diane listens to all the time, which I HATE.

But he said YES and then when we were dancing I told him I liked him a lot. He just smiled and didn't say he liked me. But then again I don't suppose he knows if he does seeing as we've never really spoken before. I was tottering around the dance floor with him, crooning 'Move Closer' like an idiot and then I knew I was gonna puke. So I had to tell him that too and he was really nice and took me outside.

In the carpark he even held my hair and rubbed my back as I puked my entire insides out onto the ground. A bit even splashed on his trainer. The SHAME. Then Emma came along and dragged me off even though she was even drunker than me. Now she's asleep and I'm lying here knowing I can never face ANYONE again. EVER.

Am I turning out just like Diane? Stumbling drunk around the streets throwing myself at men?

Oh God. I have to get away from here.

No more discos. No more cider.

Focus on my photography. My way out.

I do still think Adam is gorgeous though.

Maybe he could come with me?

My head is spinning again. so I have to go.

Shelter

Wind battered the building, hurling snow against the windows. Stephanie shivered. She'd better be able to get back to the B&B in this. Emma set two more large glasses of red wine down on the table. 'We have to go after these. Dave wants to shut and get home before the storm really hits.'

Stephanie glanced at the clock on the wall. Only quarter to nine. She'd have to get a cab back to the B&B and collect her car tomorrow. 'OK, I'll order a taxi.'

Every number she tried rang and rang and rang until she gave up.

'You can stay at mine. We can top and tail like we did when we were kids,' Emma giggled.

Stephanie smirked, 'I'm well past the age of doing that. I'll have to see if I can get a room somewhere.'

'No chance. Everywhere's shut for the season.'

She really didn't want to go back to the house. Stacey was acting so weird. But it looked like she'd have to. At least it would only be for one night. She'd sleep on the sofa. She sent Stacey a text and received a reply instantly.

OK. I'll leave your key under
the mat if I go to bed.

Stephanie shuddered. The past dragging her back again.

When they left the pub forty-five minutes later, they could barely see a couple of feet in front of them. An angry snow God was wreaking his vengeance on them tonight. Maybe they deserved it with everything they'd been doing to the planet. Clinging to each other's arm they slipped and slid along the road. By the amusement arcade opposite the beach, Emma turned left and Stephanie carried straight on, the wind and snow pummelling her now she had to face them alone. Snowflakes like icy whips flaying her face.

The waves roared and hammered against the beach. The noise and the cold and the dread about staying at the house curdled in her stomach. The nausea she'd been fighting off all evening, all day actually, wouldn't be suppressed any longer. She stumbled into the gutter and vomited wine and peanuts into the snow — retching and retching until there was nothing left. At least nobody else was out in this to see her behaving just like Diane.

'Are you okay?' A gruff voice said as the dog, Jerry, appeared from behind and sniffed at her puke. 'Jerry, away now.'

Stephanie straightened up and turned, her face burning with shame. What would he think of her? 'Thanks. I'm fine. Can't handle my drink,' she gave a forced laugh.

'No, you never could,' Adam replied.

Stephanie's face flared up even more despite the Arctic temperatures. 'Sorry I didn't recognise you the other day,' she said.

'That's okay, I didn't recognise you either. It's been a long time. We're both…different.'

Stephanie nodded, stamping on the spot to warm up. 'I better go anyway. Get indoors.' What a thing to say. 'Sorry, that was thoughtless. Where are you going? Have you got somewhere to stay?'

Adam shrugged. 'There's plenty of doorways if the chapel's locked up. I'll walk you home first.'

Stephanie smiled. Back in the day, Adam Chambers offering to walk her home would have made her year. 'Thanks.'

At the gate, she turned to face him hoping she didn't stink too badly. 'Come in. You can't stay out in this tonight.'

'Ah no, I don't think so. Stacey won't like that.'

'Stacey? Why not?'

'We've had a couple of run-ins in the past. She's not so keen on me.'

Stephanie glanced up at the house. All in darkness. 'She's gone to bed already. She won't even know. You can sneak off in the morning before she gets up.'

Adam gave a sad smile. 'Are you sure? You don't even know me anymore.'

'I'm sure. Emma would've told me if you were a psycho,' she squeezed his arm. 'Come on.'

As she slipped the key out from under the mat and they tiptoed inside, Stephanie knew he wouldn't be the only one sneaking off before Stacey got up.

Trapped

The front door clicking shut woke her. She rolled over on the sofa. The only sign Adam had been there was the cushion left on the floor under the window where he'd slept, and the empty mug from the tea Stephanie had made last night. She smiled. Finally spent the night with Adam Chambers but not in the way she'd once dreamed of. She better get going too before Stacey got up. As she stood, her head spun. She ran to the loo.

Retching again and again. But there was nothing left inside to come up. Stephanie sank down on the floor leaning against the bath. Surely she hadn't been that drunk? She'd only had a couple of glasses of wine.

After splashing her face with water, she straightened her hair and clothes. Gripped the sink as dizziness whirled through her again. Fresh air would help. She tip-toed back to the living room. The house stayed silent. Maybe she should just wait for Stacey to get up. They really did need to talk. But not now. Not when she felt so awful. She'd go back to the B&B get a couple of hours more sleep. A shower, food, a walk. Then she would have the strength to come back.

As she stood, a framed photo on the wall caught her eye. The three of them laughing and eating ice creams on Woolacombe beach. Diane had been into taking selfies long before everyone else had. Back when photos were still taken on film. Was it Diane's excitement at getting her photos back from Snappy Snaps that had sparked something in Stephanie? Whatever it was, that fire had been extinguished long ago. And anyway, everyone's a photographer in the digital age.

The day in the photo was the first time they'd had a day out to Woolacombe since Dad had left. Diane was celebrating getting a new job. They'd eaten salty chips straight from the paper in the sand dunes. Fed some to the seagulls. They could spare them now. There'd been a decomposing whale washed up right down the other end of the bay. The smell as they'd neared it had been what they'd noticed first. Diane pretended she thought it was Stephanie and Stacey who smelled. She kept running away from them into the shallows and kicking water when they tried to get close. The dark days — when Diane didn't get out of bed, or didn't come home, and there was no food in the house — seemed to have been swallowed by the bright summer sun.

Stephanie smiled. There were some good times.

But not many.

The job didn't last long. Nor the many that came after it. By the time Stephanie was entering puberty they were scraping by on benefits again. But Diane still managed to find money for booze. That's when things really went sour. She should let herself remember though that it wasn't all bad, all the time.

She reached out a finger and traced it across Diane's face in the photo, then Stacey's, then her own. Swallowed the burn in her throat. She mustn't cry now. A day out at the beach didn't really make up for it all did it? She ripped the picture down from the wall, pulled it from the frame, screwed it up and threw it across the room. Get a grip.

When she opened the front door, she was confronted by a world of white.

Mountainous drifts covered the cars parked on the road. Adam and Jerry's footprints walked away from the door in two-foot-high snow. The sky weighed heavy with more. For once it seemed the media hadn't been exaggerating. There was no way her car would get up the hills leading out of town.

She pulled the door shut and went back to the sofa. Kicked off her boots and huddled back under the quilt, scrolling on her phone to the local news.

North Devon cut off as Beast from the East hits hard. M5 Closed. Exmoor roads impassable. Many villages unreachable.

The weather was keeping her sealed up in this house.

Making sure there would be no more running away from the memories.

Maternal Instinct

From the sofa Stephanie looked up at her sister, wanting to thank her for the tea, for letting her stay, but the words were stolen by a wail that tore itself up through her throat. Her sobs were so wretched, so huge, she could barely breathe and when she felt Stacey's arms enfold her, she clung to her, let herself be rocked like a baby until the weeping died down.

'There, there. There, there,' Stacey murmured.

Nonsense words but Stephanie was soothed by them. She'd used them too, when they were little, when Stacey needed consoling after Diane, or her latest boyfriend, or both of them at once, had been on another rampage. Clearing her throat, Stephanie pulled away from Stacey's embrace. Kept her eyes cast down. She really needed to pull herself together.

'Okay?' Stacey asked.

Stephanie nodded, shuddered, and picked up her tea to give herself a moment. After a few tepid sips she put it back down again. She could only drink tea when it was scalding hot. 'Sorry. Don't know what came over me.'

Stacey rolled her eyes, 'Um, could it be that your mum died and you just came home and saw your long-lost sister for the first time in sixteen years?'

'I suppose it could be,' Stephanie said with a wan smile. Relief that Stacey was behaving a bit more normally surged through her. Maybe everything was going to be okay between them.

'Budge up,' Stacey tucked herself under the quilt too. She picked up the photo album from the floor where Stephanie had left it last night. The very first page held two pictures. One of each of them at just a day old. Looking identical.

Stacey smiled. 'We were so cute.'

Stephanie reached out, gently squeezed Stacey's forearm. 'I really am sorry you know?'

Stacey nodded. 'I know you are.' She pushed the album onto Stephanie's lap. 'I'll make us a fresh brew then I think it's probably time we talked properly. Don't you?'

Stephanie watched her walk away then flicked over to the next page of the photo album. The two of them here in this room on a rug in front of the fire. Stacey a new-born baby, Stephanie just a year old. Grinning, gripping her chubby fingers around her new sister's tiny ones. In matching pink dresses, with matching blue eyes. The photo on the page opposite was from a year or so later, matching outfits again. Stephanie cuddling Stacey on her lap on a bench down by the beach.

Stephanie shoved the photo album onto the floor. Why was she looking at photos all the time? She didn't need to be reminded of the past through the distortion of a family album. The images that people choose to present to the world. The camera does lie. Where were the photos of the fights? The neglect? The hunger and the poverty?

Bile rose in Stephanie's throat again. She leaned her head back against the sofa, swallowing it down.

It finally dawned on her.

It was nothing to do with booze.

Testing Times

Stephanie pushed past Stacey coming back with the cups of tea and rushed out the front door. There's no way she could be, is there? She counted backwards in her head to her last period. Oh God. It was just before they went on holiday at Christmas. She hadn't had a period for about ten weeks. How had she not noticed?

She slipped and stumbled through the deep snow. Her town boots not equipped for it, cold and wet seeping through her jeans and down into her socks. She'd freeze if she stayed out in this very long. But she couldn't be in the house now. Couldn't talk to Stacey now.

Stuffing her hands in her pockets she headed for the front. Maybe a shop would be open and she'd be able to buy a test. The five-minute walk to Lidl took almost fifteen as she waded through the snow. Stephanie almost cried when she saw the lights glowing inside. The relief of the warm air that rushed over her when the door swung open stilled her mind, momentarily.

She stood in the doorway for a moment letting herself thaw out. Stamped her feet to free them from the crust of icy snow.

'Excuse me, love, can I come in?'

Stephanie stood to the side to let the old man pass.

He winked at her with the bright blue eyes of his youth. 'Making the most of the free heating? Amazing how long it takes me to buy milk and bread.' He chuckled and carried on into the shop.

Stephanie followed him.

She re-emerged in dry socks and wellie boots, her wet ones in a bag for life and an expensive digital pregnancy test in her jacket pocket. By the time she reached the beach, she was freezing again. She'd have to get inside. The Wetherspoons would be open.

Inside, a few people were dotted about eating breakfasts and watching the TV news.

She drank a cup of tea and ate some toast, then headed for the toilets.

After she'd weed on the test, she sat in the cubicle with the stick in her hand staring at the blank display screen. Her stomach clenching over and over again.

What did she want it to say?

For so long she'd wanted to have a baby but hadn't allowed herself to. Knowing there was no way she could be a good mother after the example she'd been set. Telling herself that the world had too many people and it was a good thing she wasn't going to burden it with more.

But now that it might be happening, did she still feel like that?

Now she'd finally come back here to face the past, things didn't seem quite so black and white. Whatever came before didn't have to dictate what came next. Maybe she could be the kind of mum she'd always wished she'd had.

She squeezed her eyes shut. Scared to look now. The longing she'd pushed away for years surging through her.

Pictures of tiny baby feet appeared behind her closed lids. Miniature fingers curling around hers.

Stephanie shook her head. She had to stop it. Why was she doing this to herself? If it said she wasn't, then so be it.

But she sat there for a few moments more.

Then she knew she couldn't put it off any longer and opened her eyes.

She was between eight and nine weeks pregnant.

Confession

The music was so loud the bass throbbed through the door and rattled the windows. Stephanie scrabbled in her coat pocket for the door key. What was Stacey doing?

Next door poked his head out of his upstairs window, 'You better get her to turn that down. I'm sick of it.'

Stephanie nodded and hurried inside. The music pulsed through her, made her heart race. Transported her straight back to the dub parties they'd gone to in Barnstaple that last summer before she'd left. She could smell the weed. Feel the sweat as she tugged off snowy boots.

Stacey was lying on her back on the sofa, tears leaking from behind her closed eyes.

Stephanie switched the music off and sat on the floor facing her.

Stacey opened her eyes, 'I killed her. I pushed Mum off the railings into the sea.' Her voice was flat, matter-of-a-fact.

A whimper escaped from Stephanie's throat. 'What? No. What are you saying?' She couldn't mean that. There's no way. But the image of Stacey in the garden when she arrived flashed across her mind. Unhinged. She shook her head. No. No. No.

Stacey sat up. 'I did. I killed her.' Then she said it again and again and again and again until she was screaming it into Stephanie's face. Then she slumped back, panting, her mouth hanging open.

Stephanie shivered. Wrapped her arms around herself tight. She should never have come back. No wonder she'd stayed away so long. This family was too messed up to be fixed. She had to go. Get away from it all. She had to keep her baby safe from all of this.

But her body wouldn't do what her mind was telling her. She couldn't stand up. She couldn't leave again.

After a while, she broke the silence, 'You don't know what you're saying. Doing. It's grief. Shock.'

'I do know. We were drunk and she climbed up there like she always does. And I reached up to pull her back like I always do. Only this time I pushed instead of pulled. I couldn't do it anymore. I knew it was the only way I'd get free.'

By the look on her face, Stacey really believed this was true. Maybe it was. Stephanie had often wanted to shove Diane off a cliff herself. But how could Stacey trust her memory of a drunken night? She couldn't let this ruin the rest of her life. Diane was always heading for an early grave.

'Have you told anyone else this?'

Stacey shook her head, her face crumpling again. 'Like who? I haven't got any friends. Mum made sure of that.' She wailed as she curled up into a ball, tucking her knees up to her chest and burying her face in the back of the sofa.

Stephanie rubbed her back rhythmically. Not really knowing what she should do. Could do. Wanted to do.

When the sobs subsided, Stephanie pulled Stacey up to sitting, held her face in her hands. 'Stacey, she fell. You did not push her. She was drunk and she fell. You were drunk too so you can't trust what your mind is telling you. It's playing tricks. The booze. The grief. All of it means you can't know for sure.'

The hope in Stacey's eyes almost undid Stephanie but she smiled to make it really true.

Whatever happened that night, Stacey had to believe she wasn't responsible for it. If Stephanie had learned anything from coming back here, it was that memories and the truth weren't the same thing at all.

Stacey smiled tentatively back, 'Maybe you're right. It's all muddled. Sometimes I think I pushed but other times I remember pulling her back. But then I think that's a memory of all the other times I got her down from there. I just don't know anymore.' Her voice cracked on the final words.

Stephanie pulled Stacey to her feet, 'You won't ever know for definite,' she said. 'The more you focus on it the harder it will be to see. You have to just let it go.'

Then she dropped Stacey's hands, turned the music back on, just as loud as it had been before. Let Toots and the Maytals' beats and words flow through her. The lyrics from almost fifty years ago seemed made just for this moment and as she swayed and started singing quietly, she felt the pressure inside her drop.

Making room for her to breathe. To be a mother. A sister again.

She sung louder and louder and louder until her voice filled the room.

The bass filled her right up and pushed everything out of her mind.

My Last Letter
To My Dead Mother
(to be placed in the coffin)

Dear Diane,

Can't believe you died before I got the chance to tell you all the reasons why I haven't spoken to you in sixteen years. I'm sure you can guess most of them. But seeing as I'm here to say goodbye I'm going to tell you them anyway. Maybe your spirit will be able to read this on the other side?

So here goes.

The drinking. Obviously a huge one. And all that went along with that. How everything always had to be about you is another biggie.

But let's not forget all those horrible men you invited into our home when Stacey and I were growing up. All the times you didn't protect us from their drunken rampages, their insults, their wandering hands. Or that you stopped me chasing my dreams. Made me believe I'd never be good enough for any of the things I wanted to do.

I've been keeping all these toxic stories about our past in a festering box inside my head ever since I left. Getting them out and tarnishing them regularly to ensure that forgiveness would always remain forgotten. The image I've kept of you: wild eyes, screeching mouth, flailing fists. I came back here with all of this stoked right back up. Ready to get this final visit over and be gone for good. To never think of you again.

But instead I've found other images sneaking in, creeping around my defences. The walks on the crumbling cliffs and the wildflowers we brought home and pressed into bookmarks. Yesterday, I found the one I made for you saving your place in the book you'll never finish that's lying on your bedside table. I could see the three of us there snuggling up in your bed and watching films all day and night, for what seemed like weeks after Dad left.

I always believed that Dad was the good one. Compressed the few memories I have of him into a glittering diamond that I polish carefully every now and then. But even though you didn't do such a great job of being our mum, at least you never left us like he did. I suppose we should be thankful that he carried on paying the mortgage. That we weren't made homeless on top of everything else.

So now I'm finally here again and you're not.

I've found the anger I've been gripping onto for so long has been hard to cling to now that I'm here. After seeing myself shouting at you and getting all out, I find that what I really want to do is hold your hand. Plan how we can make up for the lost sixteen years. And all the years it was horrible before that. Find a way to be mother and daughter again.

But I can't. So instead, I'll just say I forgive you. I understand more now. I wish you hadn't had to die to make me realise this.

Love always,
Stephanie x

Lady Justice

Stephanie stared up at the foetus in Verity's bronze womb. She couldn't keep away from this statue and came every day to spend time with her. It was as if Verity, with her scales of justice and mighty sword held high, was telling Stephanie something about coming back here. Stephanie had passed her judgement on Diane, Stacey, her childhood, long ago. Was only coming back to mete out punishment. Although who she was punishing and for what were no longer clear.

What she'd thought she'd known for definite about her life in Ilfracombe was becoming more opaque with every passing day. Was anything we remembered ever the ultimate truth? Or just the version of it we told ourselves to make it more palatable. Make ourselves better, or worse, in our own eyes.

Then there was the motherhood to come that Verity displayed so wantonly. Stephanie had come back here to bury her mother. She hadn't expected to discover she was going to be one.

Leaning back against the railings, she stared down at the remnants of the filthy snow clogging the gutters. Closed her eyes and let her mind fill with the eerie chiming of the wind whipping through the masts of the docked sailboats. Anything to keep away what she needed to face up to. She'd have to tell Ryan he was going to be a father. Even though she knew she was never going back to him. She'd said she'd wait until the bruises on her arms faded before deciding what to do. And she had. The bruises were gone and so was he. He wouldn't want to be a dad anyway. It would involve thinking about someone other than himself. And anyway, it was a long trip from London to Ilfracombe, and this was where she was going to stay. Her baby would grow up by the sea, like she had. But she'd have a very different childhood from Stephanie's.

'Hello.'

Stephanie opened her eyes. 'Hello Adam.'

He was different. Brighter. Younger almost.

She looked down, expecting to see his little friend. 'No Jerry?'

'He's at home.' It was as if he was singing the words.

'Home? You've got somewhere to live?'

Adam nodded. A grin he couldn't suppress lifted up his whole face. For a moment, she could almost see the boy he'd been.

'That's great, Adam. Let's go get a cup of tea. I have some news as well.'

'I'm buying. Dave has given me a room in the pub and a job washing up in the kitchen.'

Seeing his head held high made tears swell in Stephanie's eyes. She blinked them back. He held out his arm and she tucked hers through it.

Stephanie glanced back up at Verity again as they walked away. Her promise of new life hidden from view now. But it was still coming.

Sisters and Mothers

When the wake in the pub ended Stephanie and Stacey headed for home, shivering in the cold wind blowing in off the sea.

'Let's go to the chapel,' Stephanie said pulling her sister to a stop.

'What for?'

'I just need to.'

Stacey shrugged and they turned around, retraced their steps back down to the harbour. At the top of the hill, they stopped and looked out across the town rising higgledy-piggledy up the hillside. Smoke curled up from many chimneys despite the sunshine glinting on windows. Waves rolled onto the harbour beach, bobbing boats around on their way there.

A gull screeched overhead then landed on the wall just a couple of feet from them.

Cocked its head to the side and stared at them with beady black eyes. Stacey went to shoo it away, but Stephanie held out a hand to still her.

'No. It's a sign.'

Stacey huffed. 'What do you mean?'

'Gulls hold the souls of those drowned at sea. Maybe it's Diane come to say her final goodbye.'

As she said that the gull jumped from the wall and floated down towards the rocks below. Then with a flap, flap, flap it propelled itself upwards. Wheeled and circled, crying and cawing, then swooped straight towards them. Passing so close, Stephanie felt the rush of air. Then it wheeled around and headed out to sea. They watched until it vanished.

Inside the chapel, the silence welcomed them in. They sat in the pew at the front. The one that had always been theirs. Rubbed their fingers over the S & S they'd carved into the seat with their compasses all those years ago.

Then Stephanie entwined her fingers with her sister's and placed Stacey's palm on her belly, holding it in place with her own.

Acknowledgements

Firstly, many thanks go to Michael Loveday who guided me through the writing of the first draft of this story in his excellent Novella-in-Flash course; and who then kindly read the final version and provided his support with a quote.

Gratitude to Kathy Fish for her wonderful Flash courses. Several of the chapters within this story were started on a course I took with her in 2019.

Earlier versions of two of the chapters were previously published in online journals and I am very grateful to the editors for believing in my work. *Peeling Away All The New Layers* appeared in Virtual Zine and *Truly Deathly* in Fictive Dream.

Big thanks to Kathy Hoyle, Matt Kendrick, and Amanda Huggins for reading an advance copy and providing their endorsements; and to all the members of the Retreat West community who share their stories in the workshops and constantly inspire me – I am in awe of what you can produce in such a short time!

Thanks to the many writers and publishers of flash fiction I have had the joy of reading over the years, you have shown me the many ways we can use this brilliant form.

And finally, thanks to you for buying a copy of my book and reading it!

Printed in Great Britain
by Amazon